The Satellite

Zoe Plait

Published by
Zoe Plait

ISBN: 0692986693
ISBN-13: 978-0692986691

First Edition, 2017
Cover Design and Illustration by Zoe Plait
Title Font by urbanfonts
Earth Image Courtesy of NASA

With utmost gratitude to all of my beloved Best Brains,
especially Trace and Frank -
I will always have a clown in the sky for you.

...

Dedicated to the Mystery Man

...

Introduction

This is a fictionalized true story about depression.

I was diagnosed with a depressive disorder when I was 12, and it didn't take long before every aspect of my life collapsed under the weight of my disease. My prolapsed mind began distorting itself beyond recognition under the influence of what eventually manifested as borderline personality disorder. It took less than a year for me to transform completely into something dark, miserable, and much less than human.

And I began hating humans as the result. At the time, nothing was more grotesque to me than reminders of my basic animal nature. I longed to be an alien, because I felt alien. I started to believe in specters and shadows to distract me from the humanity that suffocated me, and from the unbearable glass shards metastasizing in my brain. I was clinically delusional, and my beliefs consumed me.

I attempted suicide when I was 14 - unsuccessfully by conventional standards, though in a sense, the depression rotting my brain really did win the war in my head that nightmarish day. As of that moment, I was gone. Any sense of the "me" who existed prior to my diagnosis finally ceased to exist; she was demolished as of the moment she tried to take her own life. Her body survived, but her brain liquified. The delusions won.

That little girl is deceased and will never come back. In her final years, she existed only to suffer, and she sacrificed everything, never to return. Only I carried corporeally on, irreversibly changed by depression into something fundamentally new.

So the version of her that survived - me - is now telling her story, years after it ended. I still remember what it feels like to endure the pure, despairing, intolerable pain of depression she suffered in her final years; so after writing and rewriting this allegory for her terminal descent through madness, I'm finally releasing it. Her story needs to be excavated. It's too important to stay buried with her.

Every minute detail of this story fictionally (and in some moments, literally) corresponds to something that actually happened to me, beginning a decade ago as of this writing. The characters are all, to some degree, real. Depression truly is like being trapped in a small empty room in space; delusion can turn you into something you don't recognize or understand; "madness" and "purpose" are sometimes utterly indistinguishable. And although you know that the girl dies in the end, don't worry; there are still surprises to be found in this story. Joy remains in hidden places. New dimensions open up overnight. And fragments of the girl still linger, alive and at peace, in the mystery that saved me.

Zoe Plait, November 2017

Chapter 1: Awakening

She's a girl, although she doesn't know it. She has no knowledge of her name or her face or where she is because for all of her waking memory, she has lived alone on a small room-sized Satellite circling Earth in a low orbit. She awoke here one day, very young, and doesn't remember how she got here or why.

Her surroundings have been exactly the same every day since, if days could be said to exist in this vacuum within a vacuum in which she circles the Earth endlessly, grazed only weakly by pale, distant sunlight. There isn't much in her little world. The Satellite is round and confining, made of two hemispheres: to the west, or so it would look from the planet below, there is a rounded glass panel that looks out across the Universe. The glass is perfectly clear; she's never touched it, or bothered even to look out across the celestial vistas it promises.

To the opposite side of the girl's world, a thick, blood-purple metal wall curves from floor to ceiling, its top half perennially dusted over in slanted, concealing shadow, sealing it off in darkness.

On the metal wall there are three things. The first and most obvious is a large, imposing Door that stretches over the girl's head, rolling with bars and bolts, almost leering down at her. It does not open.

The second thing is a small, round hatch, hardly larger than her fist, near the bottom of the Door where exactly once daily the silent vault swings open and a spindly black hand pushes a slice of bread and a glass of water at the girl's feet. After swiftly doing this and nothing more, the hand slithers back behind the hatch in the Door without a sound.

The third thing is quite small and it terrifies the girl: a rectangular hole like a mail slot just above the center of the Door, etched in shadow, pitch black and almost humming in its mysterious silence. In her wordless language, she calls it the Evil Thing, inexplicably certain it tells lies and unspeakable secrets.

Only one other thing exists in the girl's miniature world, slumped, downtrodden, and all but forgotten: a doll, just a children's toy, neglected in the corner of the Satellite. With its green fabric flesh and striped amethyst leggings, it resembles a Halloween witch, complete with wooden broom and pointed pitch black hat. Had the girl any memories of the toy, she might have shown it more affection; it was her favorite as a little girl, and she clutched it close, her only remaining token of humanity and childhood, on the day years ago when she became trapped in this lonely little world. Memories of playing with it in her youth, of course, have been lost long ago to time and insanity, and she doesn't touch it anymore, as she has forgotten its purpose.

Apart from this, there is nothing.

Chapter 2: Invasion

Incalculable seconds and minutes and years pass, and the girl is no closer to understanding her purpose in this orbital incubator, or what the nature of the peculiar hand is, or where the ever-unopened Door leads. But even in this ignorant state, the girl must live by her instincts, urges she doesn't understand and can't control. She doesn't know even that she's an animal, but she must behave like one. The most potent human survival instinct is love, and even in her isolation, the burning desire to experience it does not escape her. Everything in the girl's body screams that she must love someone, or something, or else her unspent devotion will eat her alive from the inside, boiling furiously in her blood until she herself boils away. No fate is worse, and so ever so slowly and without her conscious knowledge, the girl spits a web of projected love blindly, thread by thread, at the only thing she knows that resembles another life form: the Hand that delivers her sustenance.

At first, she perceives it as only a hand, with just enough independent movement to be a suitable target for her affections. But she grows tired and unsatisfied with this ruse before long, her limerence unreciprocated. Time passes, and the girl realizes that the fingers on the

Hand, although talon-like and unforgiving, essentially mirror hers in function, and it dawns on her slowly and wordlessly that where there's a Hand, there's an arm. Where there's an arm there's a body, and where there's a body there's a capacity for love.

Once every cycle of the planet below, the Hand appears and brings the girl her life-saving ambrosia. And once every cycle, it slithers back into its hole behind the ominous Door just as quickly as it had appeared to crouch and wait and live a life she cannot see. But her newfound devotion demands she be a part of that other life, undoubtedly superior to her own in every way, so she sits and she waits for the Door to open and reveal to her the thing she cares about most, now a vague but unmistakably fully-formed humanoid in her imagination. Undoubtedly it must love her too; her small, undernourished mind can't permit any other worldview. No other circumstance but uniting with her lover could be worth living. So she turns her back on the glass hemisphere with its overwhelming terrestrial view, which in her mind is nothing more than a malevolent distraction from her life's only meaning: awaiting the moment the looming Door creaks open and her lover reveals itself to her. The Moon's exquisite elliptical orbits mean nothing to her, and she finds no beauty in the twinkling constellations of fiery stellar bodies that share the empty Universe with her. All is the Door.

She floats down to the floor on bare feet as she has countless times before, gently crosses her legs, and cricks her neck up expectantly.

The Door doesn't open.

She continues to wait.

…

The Earth turns on its ancient creaky axis, and hours pass. Space itself hums away in the endless darkness, existing. The girl's Halloween witch with its single remaining button eye frowns slightly at the ground as if it knows it has been abandoned. Still the Door makes no promise of coming undone.

-giveup-

Malnourished and reeling, swells of impatience well up in the girl's mind and body until for the first and far from last time, she loses control. Her vigilance finally taxes her beyond what she can withstand.

-thereisnoonethere-

Blinded by fury at this invasive thought, she snaps to her feet too quickly even to resist the impulse, and begins clawing at the Door with breaking fingers, screaming until her throat blisters. There must be something there, and she must get to it. Somehow her hands, almost with minds of their own, make their way to opposite wrists as she slams her slight frame into the Door. Jagged fingernails open her veins until the metal glistens red. Toes sticking to the floor with blood, her adrenaline finally releases and she sucks on her wounds, blaming them on the many sharp metal pieces adorning the Door. Psychosis begins to set in, and her brain rots.

-youarealone-

She glances at the Evil Thing and looks away just as quickly, feeling hateful and sick.

Nothing, not even the Evil Thing, can convince the girl that the thing behind the Door isn't as desperate to see her as she is to see it, let alone that it doesn't exist. She decides that it can't be her lover's fault that it has not shown itself to her and given her the undefined happiness she so craves; such a reality would be unlivable to her now. Welts now crawling across her wrists like cobwebs, she slowly comes to decide that some evil external force is keeping the two of them from being together.

...

It comes to her in a nightmare.

The Evil Thing has always been there and she has always seen it, although she ignores it to the best of her insanity. As a younger girl, farther back in time than she can now wakefully recall, she clawed up to it by the tips of her pale fingers using the Door's metal outcroppings. Peeking through, she saw something so heartbreaking, so mind-shatteringly devastating that she convinced herself the little window showed lies and false realities. Whatever resides within the Evil Thing, emanating its malicious pulsating darkness, she knows in her diseased little heart that it is keeping her apart from her love.

The girl awakens with a fearful jolt from her nightmare on the crimson-black floor where she had fallen, bleeding, into sleep. Dripping with terror, she laments the dream, although she can't stand to remember what she saw beyond the Evil Thing. So she cries without understanding why. The ghastly images recur the next time she sleeps, and the next, slowly feeding an idea in the neglected depths of her starving mind: somehow, the Evil Thing tells her there is no body on the other side of the Door.

But, she comes to decide slowly in her state of blossoming madness, that doesn't mean there is no mind there.

Chapter 3: The Mission

Wasn't the girl aware instinctively of something greater than herself that exists inside her? Even a human consciousness as limited as hers is expansive enough to fill more than a few pounds of simple flesh, it seems. Her love has more power, more luminosity, more gravity than the confines of her physical being; and so the girl becomes aware of the concept of a soul.

And if she has one, so must the Thing behind the Door.

So the Thing is alive, she decides, just not in any tangible form. It is a hovering consciousness, untethered to a fragile body, able only to manipulate the Hand that delivers her sustenance in the absence of corporeal existence. The Evil Thing, then, was joyously wrong: her lover might not exist, but it was certainly real.

...

Reinvigorated by this discovery for a time, the girl's mind continues to heave silently in the darkness of her little world. Existence continues on its ambivalent course through the rest of the empty Universe, and still the girl does nothing but wait, and sleep. Occasionally the doll almost melting in the corner of the ship catches her eye, and the girl feels the whispering edge of a rageful enviousness rotting a hole in her heart; so she pleads unconsciously with the Universe to switch their two bodies, girl and doll, so that her misery ends and she finally feels the blissful nothingness, always just out of reach, that oblivion promises. In her human form, she is susceptible to heartbreak and despair and relentless unremitting depressive pain; a doll feels no such misery. This death wish fantasy is always dashed quickly, however, as the girl turns her stoic vigilance back to the greedy Door, always the Door.

So, keeping only the company of the witch and the walls of her little Satellite, restlessness slowly chips away at the girl's fragmenting mind as the Door continues to do nothing but glare back at her, unloving.

...

Time passes, and slowly, another instinct begins to take over the young girl, in the excruciating emptiness of her microcosm: the need for a purpose in life, a greater calling to occupy her time and soul. In the vacuum of her little spaceship, no such purpose makes itself known to her, so out of necessity and madness she creates one. Influenced heavily by her masochistic tendencies, a plan begins to form in the sickness infecting her brain, so amplified by depression that she can't ignore it.

If the Thing she loves so much needs a body, she'll give it the only one she has.

Chapter 4: Misery

For countless years the Halloween witch has sat untouched in the farthest corner of the Satellite from the Door, where the girl doesn't have to burn in envy of it. Now, for the first time, the doll gives her an idea.

When the Hand comes around next, she is ready. Still mostly unfamiliar with physical pain and its causes, she doesn't grimace, hardly screams as she snaps the broom to pieces and uses its sharp, splintered end to saw a bleeding finger off of her left hand. Wood scrapes flesh, then bone, then flesh again, then nothing at all as the finger falls lightly into her lap, leaving the freshest of many future crimson stains on her thin and threadbare white dress. As the Hand behind the Door delivers her food and drink, she offers it the piece of her own body.

Another day, another finger.

Her toes go next, then one leg below the knee, and her left ear. Each piece is more excruciating than the last to saw off, and blood now drenches the floor of the small Satellite. As her throat blisters from screaming, the sound becomes less bloodcurdling and more familiar in her ears, like the beautiful musical soundtrack to her sacrifice.

With each body part that she saws off, the girl uses thread from the October doll to stitch together a fabric piece to use in place of her missing flesh. Without the technical skill to reproduce small and complex parts, she replaces her left hand with a spindly fabric tube that comes to a sharp point where fingers should be; her toes meet the same fate. Stuffing herself with blood-soaked cotton, she calmly moves on to the next part, anatomically malformed, methodically insane.

As if gaining awareness that they are being murdered, the girl's remaining human pieces begin to rebel before her unholy mission is halfway complete, their unified animal protest amplifying in her mind for every sister part that is sacrificially severed. The physical pain intensifies, and her psyche rends itself. Her brain, teeming with disease but also with inherent humanity, screams and pleads with her to stop shredding its body.

Many times, she almost listens. But in the end, she never does.

Chapter 5: Human

It's now, when the girl is made mostly of thread and fabric, that an entirely new thing enters her deranged life for the first time since the Hand gave her the gift of her first meal. On the other side of the glass that separates the girl from the Universe's mostly empty void that means so little to her, an object suspends in the far distance. She discovers it out of the corner of her eye upon awakening on the dried-blood metal floor and commands herself to pay it no further attention in favor of greedily watching the Door, sure that her blood sacrifice would quench its thirst very soon, and it would open.

However, a few of her original parts still remain, and they have joined together for the purpose of survival, their humanity strengthened in the face of her self-massacring final act; they are driven by ravenous curiosity, desperate that this new thing might somehow save them.

So, for the first time in epochs, and without her conscious instruction, she turns her back on the Door.

Something moves inside the New Thing.

A monster, it seems, flickers past one of the new object's windows. Despite herself, she squints to get a better look, and takes a tentative step across the crime-scene floor of her world toward the neglected vista outside.

Chapter 6: Mystery

The girl observes with captive fear as the monster moves on two jointed fleshy stilts, disgusting limbs protruding in opposite directions from its torso, which is wider and taller than her own. It appears to her as if something dark and furry has died upon its head, and a hole rots open near the bottom of its face, a crescent turned upward like the Moon she so despises.

Horrified but transfixed now, the girl watches the movements of the monster, which is painted in strokes of warm maroons and thriving oranges to which she's never borne witness before. Life appears colorful on the other side of the New Thing's spaceship, which is larger and more inviting than her own, with glints of violet, gold, and scarlet abounding. As thoughts of the thing behind the Door become overshadowed for the first time in unknowable years, the girl realizes her body balances on stilts much like the monster's. The rotting hole in her head, though its crescent faces downward, is unmistakably of the same nature; her arms protrude much like his do.

As familiarity begins to unfold in the few remaining working parts of the girl's mind, something she has never experienced before washes over her: a sensation of rejuvenating heat, spreading slowly from her still-human chest outward through her doll's arms, although until now she has been unfamiliar with anything but the bone-chilling cold of her world. Heartbeat to heartbeat, she feels unwittingly connected to this person, the only other one she has ever seen, hearing for the first time the infantile song of interhuman tenderness playing at the corners of her starved mind.

This creature, too, must surely have a soul, and she feels it with her own.

Chapter 7: The Void

In a moment of self-destructive purpose, however, the girl snaps her narrow attention back to the Door. Internally screaming at the strange Man's gift of warmth now radiating from her traitorous body, she rips out her own heart as it beats for the last time.

...

From the girl's now completely twisted point of view, her hellish plan is a success. Supposedly, a formless creature, one for which she feels an undying love, has been piecing together her sacrificed lumps of flesh day by day on the other side of the Door, and now manipulates a bastardized version of her body with its floating consciousness. And, she has no doubt, as soon as her last part is sawed off and offered, the Hand will finally be able to open the cursed metal Door that has haunted the girl for a lifetime, and reveal itself. Eternally by the Hand's side, the girl will no longer be a prisoner on her little Satellite, instead drenched in blissful devotion to her true love, a doll and a monster that used to be a girl.

Finally, the time comes for the girl to saw off her head.

-don'tdoit-

She sightlessly installs the sickly greenish fabric head onto her poor, pencil-thin neck, and peering through a single button eye, she holds out her lifeless human head on shaking doll's arms to the small hole at the bottom of the Door.

The Hand doesn't come.

The girl waits.

The Hand doesn't come.

-lookattheNewThing-

After a few moments the girl slowly sits, eternity hanging in the balance, stuffing leaking from between the stitches in her broken backward knees.

-lovetheNewThing-

The Hand doesn't come.

The girl sleeps.

She awakens cold and wet with no memory of falling unconscious. It seems the Hand had come while the usual nightmares had tortured her in her wretched sleep. However, for the first time in her small, sad life, the water is tipped over and the bread is soaked, inedible. Frozen in disorientation, she barely registers the cold of her only daily water on her fabric skin.

As she realizes the Hand's mistake, her undead breath begins to quicken: never before has it tipped her water over. The Hand is incapable of imperfection, she reasons in her madness, so spilling the water must have been intentional.

It's a sign, she's sure of it. She has sacrificed the final part of herself and the Hand is coming.

And so the girl waits for her first and final lover to present to her its beautiful manifest self. Never before has she been filled with so much maniacally obsessive determination, even as repressed thoughts of the New Thing escalate from a whisper to a scream in the back of her emaciated mind.

But the Door doesn't open, and the Hand doesn't come.
She waits.

-don'tlovetheHAND-

She sleeps.
…
With her every small movement, every twist and turn under the torturous influence of the nightmares, the girl's fabric body unravels slightly. She is literally coming apart at the seams, stuffing leaking from her every unraveling part and poorly stitched suture. Whatever evil life force keeps her breathing without a heartbeat begins to decay as her physical form does. The Hand continues to rest infuriatingly dormant behind the Door, which does not open.

-lovetheHUMAN-

An unknowable amount of time passes, and the girl is delirious. She cannot wait any longer for her lover to show itself, and she bursts out more violently than ever at the Door. As she throws herself furiously against its unforgiving metal leer, its many mysterious metal bolts snag her fabric skin and tear out her stitches. As she unravels, she revels in one final outburst of sweet masochism and claws at the Door with inhuman strength. Fragments of her new body hanging from the wall, her mind dissolves like the wet cotton it is and whatever lingering consciousness remains in her deranged mind begins to dim at the corners of her fading vision.

...

She lies facedown and motionless on the cold floor, unstirring, unstirred. The Earth spins on its ancient creaky axis. Her life drains away quickly - or slowly, she does not know - and in a final desperate attempt to live to see the Door open, she does the one thing she vowed never to do: she looks up.

-*LOVE THE HUMAN*-

Chapter 8: Fall

The New Thing is very close now. While the girl-doll was dying, it drifted ever closer, its course set but its mysterious intentions unknown to her. The Man now stands very near to the other side of a window of his orbital home, close enough that she can see his breath leaving a gentle pulsing fog on the glass. Blood pumps heartily through his veins, giving his cheeks a youthful cherry pink glow. His hair, his skin, his eyes - all seem to have grown much older in the time it took her to unravel, as if they had lovingly memorized every detail of the planet below, and learned to mirror the deep human blues of Earth's swirling skies and oceans over a lifetime.

Once again, despite herself, she finds loving him to be criminally easy; his body, mind, and breath all mirror hers too closely to ignore. Their inherent commonalities beg for her affection, even in her monstrous doll form. Tangible and irrefutably real, his existence depends upon no imagination, no psychosis; and most critically of all, she knows that his love asks for no pain or sacrifice - nothing at all in return.

He gazes at the girl with an odd expression she has no way of recognizing; never before has she had occasion to feel the compassion playing across his soft features now. And with her final breath, she screams at the love she feels for him.

...

The girl dies, but the doll dreams.

In her comatose purgatory, neither dead nor alive, she hallucinates waking up wholly human again in the spot where her body died, dress untorn and unstained with years' worth of self-spilled blood. She floats to her feet, weightless and fully alive, to find the Man standing where she had left him in her last moment. In her dream, she can hear his heart beating, the only sound she's ever heard apart from the silent hum of the apathetic Universe and her own screams.

Despite herself, she loves him.

As she gazes with newfound wonderment into his tidal eyes, she realizes they don't look directly back at her own, but instead at something in the distance just over her shoulder.

He nods and she turns.

...

It has always been there and she has always seen it. The Evil Thing perches maliciously just above the Door, out of reach for her doll body, but perfectly at eye level in her dream-restored human form. Oddly unafraid with the new Man's warm gaze upon her back, the girl drifts weightlessly across her clean and sparkling tiny world to the Evil Thing.

...

The room on the other side of the ventilation hole in the wall is very small and very dark. It takes her eyes a moment to adjust to its blackness after experiencing the brilliant light from the Man's Satellite. Walls painted the same bloody pinkish as the metal confines of her world, only a few inconspicuous objects rest on the floor of the little closet on the other side of the Door: stores of dehydrated bread and water, a small hydrator, an air circulation device, and a limp, spindly black hand that plugs into the wall, sparking, motionless, and broken on the floor. Apart from this, there is nothing.

...

When the girl turns back to her world, the dream turns into a nightmare.

A young body, small and effeminate, lies in a bloody dismembered pile in the corner of the Satellite. Layers upon layers of dried blood pool on the floor, fingers lie scattered everywhere, and small mounds of flesh cling to the walls, stuck from being violently propelled there over weeks and months. All the girl's accumulated years of screaming begin to ring through the room where she killed herself, piece by piece, for a lover that never existed.

Chapter 9: Home

She awakens, bent and broken, her doll's body one undone stitch away from obliterated lifelessness. Her vision and breath fade in and out, her mind tortured and fragmented nearly beyond repair by the dawning comprehension of the masochistic act she devoted her life to committing. As the new Man gently seals an airtight passage to the transparent wall of her ship and drills a door-sized hole in the glass, the girl clings to the awareness of two things: her screaming hatred for the Man who destroyed her love for the thing behind the Door, and the infinitely stronger love that burns in her heart for him and his humanity.

Stepping softly into her World - the only other inhabitant it has seen in a lifetime - the stranger gingerly lifts the decaying doll in his lovely lined hands, cradling her so close to his chest that she can hear his heartbeat, real this time, not just a figment of her dreams. She tries to scream her protest but finds her vocal chords are split and broken. She squirms in his palms in an attempt to escape, but her severely damaged fabric limbs are taxed too far and will not operate. Refusing until her last conscious breath to give her fate over to the Man who so lovingly murdered her dreams, she steals one final glance at the Door. It does not open.

He sings her into unconsciousness, a mystery man and a broken girl-doll, and carries her home.

End

ABOUT THE AUTHOR

Zoe Plait is the author of the website Miss Misery (missmisery.blog), where she chronicles her adventures with depression, anxiety, and borderline personality disorder. She is currently studying psychology and neuroscience in Boulder, CO, and plans to become a PhD neuroscientist at the University of California, San Francisco.

www.ingramcontent.com/pod-product-compliance
Lightning Source LLC
Chambersburg PA
CBHW070654130626
46555CB00006B/2878